BEANIE

BEANIE

by Ruth
and
Latrobe Carroll

NEW YORK *Henry Z. Walck, Incorporated* 1953

To

Arthur Stupka, Park Naturalist of the Great Smoky Mountains National Park.

The Alexanders of the Cataloochee Ranch in the Great Smokies.

Glenn Messer of Hemphill Valley, and his mountain-farm family.

The Mosers of Buckeye Cove.

And to Maggie, the bear, who showed rather clearly what she thought of our research by trying to bite off our noses.

Beanie wanted a puppy. He wanted a puppy more than any-
thing in the world. He was the only one in the Tatum family
who didn't have a pet.

His father had a pet, a dog named Sour Bone. His mother had a pet, a fat cat named Cookie. His older brother Buck had a pet, a dog named Nip. His older sister Serena had a pet, a cat named Barbie. His brother Irby had a pet, a dog named Whizz. His sister Annie Mae had a pet, a kitten named Pinky Nose.

Beanie had begged and begged and begged for a puppy. His father had kept saying he was too young to take good care of a pet. But Beanie kept hoping and hoping and hoping to get one on his birthday.

As months and months and months went by, and his birthday came closer and closer and closer, he hoped harder and harder and harder.

At last it *was* his birthday. His mother gave him a bright shirt and a pair of overalls. He put on the shirt and he pulled on the overalls and he smiled. They were a little too big for him. But he was getting a little bigger every day, so he would soon fill them out.

Buck gave him a make-believe gun. Beanie aimed it at Sour Bone and said, "You're a big old bear. Bang, Bang, BANG!"

Serena gave him a cap. He put it on. He straightened his back and he straightened his neck and stood taller.

Annie Mae gave him a big fat honey-candy bar. When he saw it his tongue tip came out and ran around a corner of his mouth. He felt too full of breakfast to eat it—too full of streaky bacon and eggs and hot biscuits and gravy and milk and apple sauce. So he poked it down into a left-hand pocket.

His father's gift was the best of all. A PUPPY!

As soon as Beanie saw him he gave a happy whoop. He jumped and he jumped and he jumped up and down—and the little dog jumped and jumped and jumped up and down, too.

The puppy was fat and gay. He looked like a ball of wool and he bounced like a ball of rubber. He had eyes like bright brown buttons and a damp black sniffing nose.

Beanie patted him and smoothed him. The puppy licked his hand. Beanie laughed.

Now the littlest Tatum of all had the littlest pet of all.

Then Irby brought out his present—a collar for the new puppy. Beanie fastened it around the little dog's neck.

Pretty soon he asked his father, "Pa, what's my pup's name?"

His father didn't know.

"I'll think and I'll think till I think of a name," said Beanie. "But till I think of a name for my pup I'll call my pup just 'Pup.'"

Beanie was sure his shirt and his overalls and his gun and his cap and his candy and his puppy and his puppy's collar were the best gifts in the world. He did not want to share them with his brothers and his sisters. He wanted to keep them all for himself.

He was afraid that Irby would borrow his shirt and his overalls and his cap. He was afraid that Annie Mae would want to play with his gun. He was afraid that, if he offered his candy to his brothers and his sisters, they would take so many bites, there wouldn't be a single bite left for him.

He didn't want them to play with his puppy because he was hoping his puppy would love him better than anybody else.

He picked up his gun and he picked up his pup and he went into his mother's and father's bedroom. He crawled under their big bed. It was low, but he had enough room under there because he was thin in a string-bean sort of way.

He wiggled close to the center of the wall so nobody could see him. He was hiding from his family.

The puppy didn't want to lie down and hide, he wanted to play. He was a bundle of wiggles. Beanie's hands tried to hold him still.

The windows were open. Beanie could hear noises. He lay on his stomach and listened.

"Woof-woof-woof!" Beanie knew what that barking was about. Beanie's father's dog, Sour Bone, was driving the cows to the gate, so Beanie's mother could milk them.

Stomp-stomp-stomp. Whinny-whinny-whinny. Beanie knew the horse was stamping and whinnying because the horse heard Buck getting him some ears of corn out of the corncrib.

Siss-siss-siss. That was the gentle sish of water falling on the cabin porch. Serena was watering the flowers in the rows of bright red cans on the front-porch railing.

"We-e-e, we-e-e, we-e-e." Beanie knew the pigs were squealing because they saw his brother Irby coming to feed them.

Swish-swish-swish. Annie Mae was sweeping the hearth.

Clup. . . . Clup. . . . Clup. His father was chopping up a big old log, for stovewood.

"Kut-kut-kut, ka-*da*-kut. Kut-kut-kut, ka-*da*-kut." A hen had laid an egg and was talking about it.

Pat-pat-pat. Annie Mae's feet were patting. She was running out of the cabin to hunt for the new egg.

All those noises told Beanie that everybody on the mountain farm was busy. Everybody was working—everybody but Beanie. He knew he had a job to do. His job was to carry stovewood to the kitchen.

"I won't tote wood on my birthday," he whispered to his pup. "I won't, I won't, I *won't*. I'll run away with you, just for a while. I'll run away with my shirt and my overalls and my gun and my cap and my candy and you."

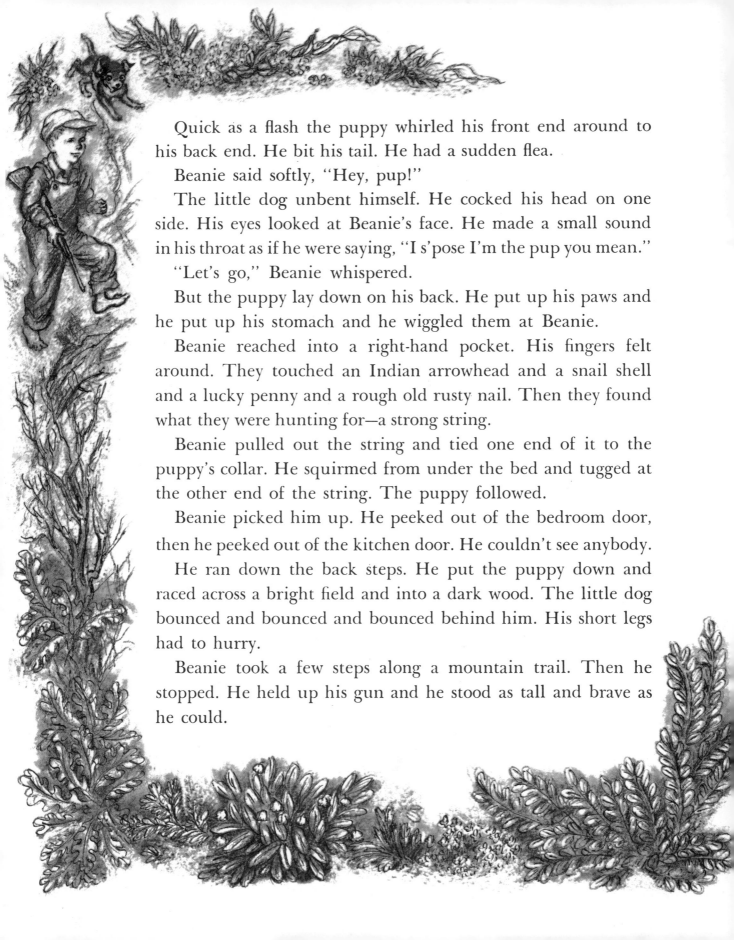

Quick as a flash the puppy whirled his front end around to his back end. He bit his tail. He had a sudden flea.

Beanie said softly, "Hey, pup!"

The little dog unbent himself. He cocked his head on one side. His eyes looked at Beanie's face. He made a small sound in his throat as if he were saying, "I s'pose I'm the pup you mean."

"Let's go," Beanie whispered.

But the puppy lay down on his back. He put up his paws and he put up his stomach and he wiggled them at Beanie.

Beanie reached into a right-hand pocket. His fingers felt around. They touched an Indian arrowhead and a snail shell and a lucky penny and a rough old rusty nail. Then they found what they were hunting for—a strong string.

Beanie pulled out the string and tied one end of it to the puppy's collar. He squirmed from under the bed and tugged at the other end of the string. The puppy followed.

Beanie picked him up. He peeked out of the bedroom door, then he peeked out of the kitchen door. He couldn't see anybody.

He ran down the back steps. He put the puppy down and raced across a bright field and into a dark wood. The little dog bounced and bounced and bounced behind him. His short legs had to hurry.

Beanie took a few steps along a mountain trail. Then he stopped. He held up his gun and he stood as tall and brave as he could.

He knew there were bears in the Great Smoky Mountains where he lived. Little black wild bears. Middle-sized black wild bears. GREAT BIG BLACK WILD BEARS.

"I'm a big old bear hunter," he said to his puppy. "And you're my big old bear dog. You'll run all over the mountains. You'll stick out your nose till it smells a bear. You'll bark and you'll run and you'll find that old bear and you'll bite him. And then I'll come runnin' and shoot him, bang, bang, BANG."

The puppy looked up. He twitched an ear. A thin asking sound came squeezing out of his throat. He lifted a puzzled paw and put it down. His tail wagged almost three times—the last wag was just half a wag.

Beanie tucked in his shirt and pushed up an overalls strap that had slipped off his shoulder. He closed his fingers firmly round his gun. He cocked his cap on one side. He poked his fingers down into a left-hand pocket and felt the good fatness of his honey-candy bar. He gave a come-on-puppy whistle.

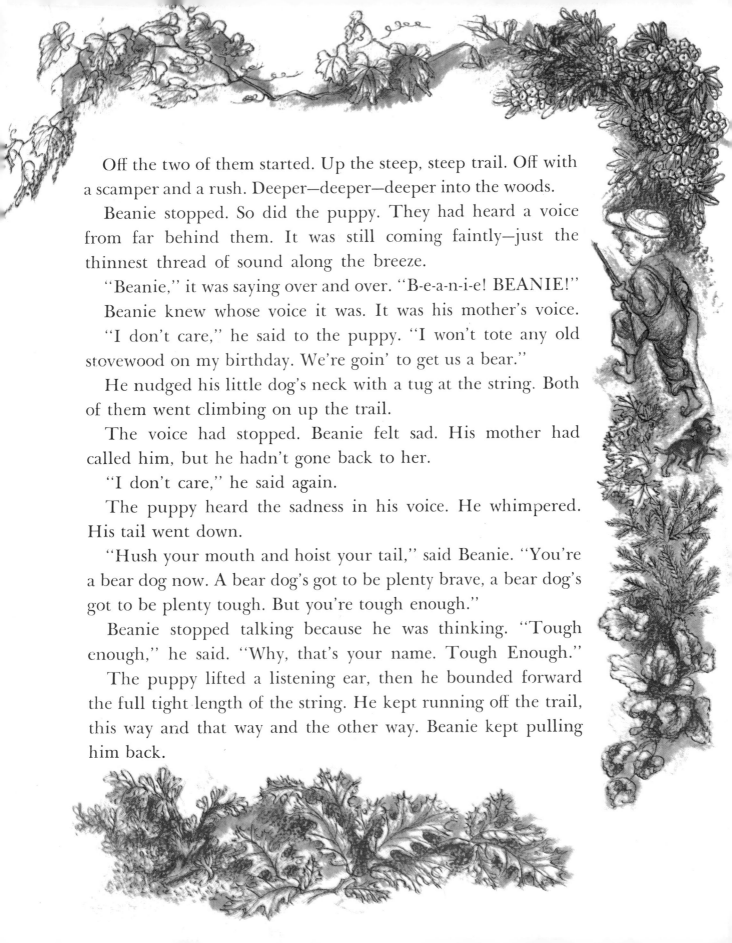

Off the two of them started. Up the steep, steep trail. Off with a scamper and a rush. Deeper—deeper—deeper into the woods.

Beanie stopped. So did the puppy. They had heard a voice from far behind them. It was still coming faintly—just the thinnest thread of sound along the breeze.

"Beanie," it was saying over and over. "B-e-a-n-i-e! BEANIE!"

Beanie knew whose voice it was. It was his mother's voice.

"I don't care," he said to the puppy. "I won't tote any old stovewood on my birthday. We're goin' to get us a bear."

He nudged his little dog's neck with a tug at the string. Both of them went climbing on up the trail.

The voice had stopped. Beanie felt sad. His mother had called him, but he hadn't gone back to her.

"I don't care," he said again.

The puppy heard the sadness in his voice. He whimpered. His tail went down.

"Hush your mouth and hoist your tail," said Beanie. "You're a bear dog now. A bear dog's got to be plenty brave, a bear dog's got to be plenty tough. But you're tough enough."

Beanie stopped talking because he was thinking. "Tough enough," he said. "Why, that's your name. Tough Enough."

The puppy lifted a listening ear, then he bounded forward the full tight length of the string. He kept running off the trail, this way and that way and the other way. Beanie kept pulling him back.

As they went up and up and up they passed trees and flowers and blossoming shrubs.

They passed the tulip tree, the white oak, the locust, the laurel, the Indian pink, the bluet—up and up and up.

They passed the hemlock, the birch, the sugar maple, the flame azalea, the paint brush, the Christmas fern—up and up and up.

They passed the sourwood, the red oak, the beech, the buckeye, the columbine, the galax—up and up and up.

They kept smelling fine smells—cool smells and warm smells, damp smells and dry smells, sweet ferny smells and hemlock smells and earthy smells and blossomy smells—so many good deep-forest smells.

They panted, huff-huff-huff. Their feet went scuff-scuff-scuff. Those huffs and those scuffs were the only sounds except for bird voices close by and far away.

A thrush was singing "O, veery, veery, veery, veery." A blue jay was screaming "Ja-a-a-y, ja-a-a-y!" And a junco was scolding "*Tsip, tsip, tsip,*" because Beanie and the puppy were passing near her nest.

"Little old puppy dog," said Beanie, "we're a long, long ways from home."

A gust of wind was rustling the forest leaves.

All of a sudden, Beanie and Tough Enough stopped. They had heard frightening sounds: Skreek, skreek, *skree-ee-k.*

"Yow!" Beanie yelled.

"Yipe!" the puppy yipped.

A few long listening seconds went by. Beanie held his breath. Another wave of wind went swishing through the woods.

Skreek, *skree-ee-k* went the skreeking again.

"YOW!" Beanie yelled again.

"YIPE!" the puppy yipped again.

Beanie stared and stared all around. Ahead, in some shadows, he saw queer streaks. They were crooked. They were dead-white.

After a moment the skreekings came again—but this time, they didn't scare Beanie. He knew just what they were. The wind was making a dry branch rub against another dry branch, and that's what the noises were.

"Yonder's that old dead thunder tree," Beanie said to the puppy. "Lightnin' hit it and killed it."

He began to move forward. Tough Enough followed him along the steep, steep trail.

"I've never been past that old thunder tree," Beanie said. "Pa told me never to go past it because I'd sure get lost in the thickety woods. But we're climbin' past it right now. I can still see the trail. We're not goin' to get lost. No. We're not."

Tough Enough sat down and scratched his neck.

"Stop scratchin', bear dog, and start smellin'," said Beanie. "Go on and smell out a bear."

Tough Enough *was* smelling, but not smelling out a bear. He was sniffing at Beanie's bare toes as if he loved them.

At last he took his nose away and aimed it along the trail. He ran ahead as far as the string would let him. He was pointing his nose at a cave.

"Lan's alive!" Beanie whispered. "I reckon there's a big old bear in there."

Both of them went close. The cave was a deep hole under great rocks. Moss and ferns half hid it. A damp mushroomy smell came breathing out of it.

Beanie stooped and peeked in. Near the cave's mouth he could see some dim rock walls. Farther in, he couldn't see a thing.

The puppy led the way in. He was frisking and prancing. But Beanie followed slowly.

"It's gettin' darker and darker," he said in a shaky voice.

His feet were giving him trouble. They didn't want to carry him along.

Far, far back in the darkness something was moving. Something quick. Something black.

"YOW!" Beanie yelled.

"YIPE!" the puppy yipped.

Beanie tried to run, but his feet just wouldn't move.

The black thing came closer. Closer. Now Beanie saw it was just a small thing, a zig-zig-zagging thing.

"It's an old bat," he said. "Nothing but a flitter-skitter old bat."

He led his puppy out of the cave.

As they went pushing on up the trail, Beanie began to sing. He was singing a Tatum song his grandmother had taught him:

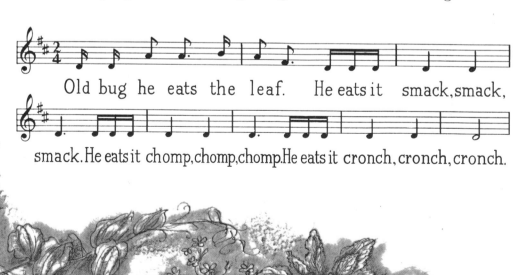

Old bug he eats the leaf. He eats it smack, smack, smack. He eats it chomp, chomp, chomp. He eats it cronch, cronch, cronch.

Old bug he eats the leaf, But he's got to find it first.

He's a - crawl-in' for his supper, Keeps a -

crawl-in' for his supper-That-old - bug.

Old blue jay eats the bug,
He eats him smack, smack, smack.
He eats him chomp, chomp, chomp.
He eats him cronch, cronch, cronch.
Old jay he eats the bug,
But he's got to find him first.
He's a-flyin' for his supper,
Keeps a-flyin' for his supper—
That—old—jay.

Old fox he eats the jay,
He eats him smack, smack, smack.
He eats him chomp, chomp, chomp.
He eats him cronch, cronch, cronch.
Old fox he eats the jay,
But he's got to catch him first.
He's a-jumpin' for his supper,
Keeps a-jumpin' for his supper—
That—old—fox.

Ruth Carroll

Now Beanie and Tough Enough were zig-zagging along under rhododendron bushes—bushes with dark green leaves and big rose-purple blossoms. The bushes met overhead and made a sort of crooked tunnel.

On and on went Beanie and Tough Enough. On and on and on.

The trail was growing so faint, it was hardly a trail at all. It led Beanie and his puppy out of the leafy tunnel and through a strip of woods. It ended at the edge of a meadow that went sloping up, up, up to a grassy mountain top. The meadow was dotted all over with clumps of bushes.

Beanie and Tough Enough climbed and climbed the steep green slope till they were tired.

Beanie sat down close to a great big bush. He laid his gun on the grass beside him.

His full-of-breakfast feeling was all gone. He reached into a left-hand pocket and pulled out his honey-candy bar and peeled off the wrapping. The candy was soft and squidgy. He took a delicious bite.

The puppy came wiggling close. He put his paws on Beanie's knee. He whined. His mouth reached for the candy.

Beanie pulled off a small piece and gave it to him. The puppy ate it up in a sudden way. His eyes were dancing. Right from his nose to his tail tip he was wiggling and squirming. Every bit of him was begging for more candy.

But in a moment he turned around fast. The hairs on his back and his neck bristled up. He was aiming his nose at the nearby bush. "Gr-r-r-r-r," he growled.

Now Beanie heard a mysterious noise. It was a rustle-rustle-rustle. It came from the other side of the bush.

He scrambled to his feet. As soon as he was standing he saw what the puppy was growling at. Beanie didn't yell. He didn't make the slightest sound. He was too surprised.

He didn't move. He couldn't.

He was staring into sharp brown eyes that stared back. They were peeking around the bush.

Those eyes were in a face. A hairy face. The mouth was partly open. Beanie could see sharp teeth.

He was looking at a bear. Its sniffing nose was wobbling. He was sure he knew what it wanted. It wanted his honey candy.

It came closer.

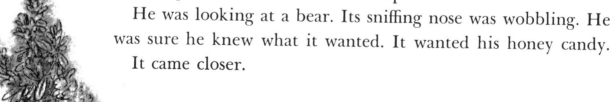

"Yap, yap, yap," went Tough Enough. He made a dash at the bear. He was trying to keep it away from Beanie.

"Come back or you'll get killed!" Beanie shouted. He dropped his candy bar. He picked up the puppy. He turned and he ran and he ran and he ran.

Ruth Carroll

He was racing toward the edge of the forest, back toward the place where the homeward trail began. At least, he hoped he was running toward that place. He knew the trail was so faint that it would be hard to find.

He glanced back over his shoulder. The bear wasn't coming after him. Not yet. It was still in the same place.

He stopped a few feet away from the edge of the woods. Now he was near a narrow clearing that cut deep into the forest. Was that where the trail began? He thought so.

As he turned around to watch the bear, the puppy in his arms gave a wiggle. Beanie almost dropped him. He tucked him inside his shirt and buttoned him in and held him with one hand. But he didn't take his eyes off the bear.

It had eaten up his candy and it was licking its mouth. Then its tongue went sliding over Beanie's gun. It was looking for more candy.

Next, it took the gun in its jaws, gave it an angry shake, and dropped it. It lifted its head and pointed its nose. It was aiming its nose straight at Beanie and the puppy.

Beanie didn't wait a second more. Off he started. He went running along in the clearing—the clearing he hoped was the beginning of the trail.

"First my candy," he thought to himself, "then my gun, then my pup and me. We're *next.*"

Weeds switched his feet. Leaves slapped his head and his shoulders. Branches scratched him. His heart was thumping, his breath was coming in gasps.

Was he on the right trail? He didn't think so now. Was the bear following him? He didn't know. But soon he got so tired that he had to stop.

He stood till he got back his breath. And as he stood he patted and smoothed Tough Enough, who was having a small fit of the wiggles.

Then Beanie went on again. He was looking for the leafy tunnel through the rhododendron bushes. But he didn't even see any rhododendron bushes.

He heard a far-off crackling. It sounded like some heavy animal pushing through underbrush.

"It's that bear comin' after us," he whispered.

He started off again as fast as he could go. Blackberry briers tore at his overalls. A sharp twig knocked off his cap. He didn't stop to pick it up.

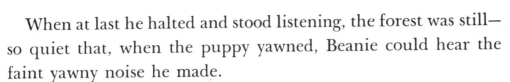

When at last he halted and stood listening, the forest was still—
so quiet that, when the puppy yawned, Beanie could hear the
faint yawny noise he made.

Beanie began to look for the trail again. He went this way and
he went that way and he went the other way. But he couldn't
see a sign of the trail.

"We're lost," he said to the puppy. "We're plumb lost." But
he went on just the same.

At last, as he looked toward some locust trees, the forest seemed
a little brighter there.

"It must be the edge of the woods over yonder," he said. "I
reckon a cliff drops off there. Reckon, if I scrouge right close to
the edge I'll get a view. If I can just only see where we're at, we
can get goin' home."

He began to make his way toward that brightness.

When he knew he must be almost at the edge he stopped. Then
slowly and carefully he began to move forward. He was inching
across a grassy hump like a green pillow. Trees were hanging
their leafy screens all around him.

He leaned forward. He was hoping for a view. He moved one
of his feet—pushed it nearer the edge, then still nearer. . . .

Suddenly he was falling—falling and grabbing at the air with
both hands. The green pillow under his feet had given way.

He didn't drop very far. He landed with a bump on a rocky shelf below—landed sitting down. The jolt threw the puppy out of his shirt—out and spinning, spinning, spinning down.

Beanie watched his puppy fall—watched him wiggling and pawing as he turned over and over. He saw him land in a clump of bushes, he heard his terrified "YIPE!"

Out of those bushes the puppy came pushing and twisting and squeezing. He struggled to his feet. Then he ran into the woods below. Beanie couldn't see him any more.

"Here pup, here pup, here pup!" he shouted. He whistled and he whistled and he whistled. But the little dog didn't come back.

"He's gone," Beanie said. "My puppy's gone."

He felt like crying. But he swallowed a lump in his throat and rubbed his eyes with his fists.

And now, for the first time since his fall, he took a long look at the valley beneath.

"Lan's alive!" he said. "I know right where I'm at."

Down below lay Sourwood Cove, his home valley. He could see the Tatum farm. He could even see the Tatum cabin.

"But how am I goin' to get home?" he asked himself. "Can I climb down?"

He looked at the steep rocks below and he knew he couldn't climb down.

He couldn't move far to the left, along the rock shelf he was

on. He couldn't move far to the right. On both sides of him that shelf narrowed till there wasn't any shelf at all.

"Well, *up* is the only way," he said to himself. "Now if I can just only skitter up like a squirrel. . . ."

Over and over and over again he tried to climb the rocks above. Over and over and over he slipped back.

"Whee-ee-ew!" he panted. "How in the world can I ever get home—to my ma and my pa and Buck, and Serena and Irby and Annie Mae, and Sour Bone and Nip and Cookie, and Whizz and Barbie and Pinky Nose? How *can* I?"

The sun had climbed higher. Waves of heat were dancing around Beanie. He felt hot, he felt thirsty, he felt very hungry.

"I've just got to perten up," he said to himself. "I reckon if I sing I'll perten up.".

He began to sing part of his Tatum song:

> Old bobcat eats the fox,
> He eats him smack, smack, smack.
> He eats him chomp, chomp, chomp.
> He eats him cronch, cronch, cronch.
> Old bobcat eats the fox,
> But he's got to catch him first.
> He's a-huntin' for his supper,
> Keeps a-huntin' for his supper—
> That—old—cat.
>
> Old bear he eats the cat,
> He eats him smack, smack, smack.
> He eats him chomp, chomp, chomp.
> He eats him cronch, cronch, cronch.
> Old bear he eats the cat,
> But he's got to catch him first.
> He's a-sniffin' for his supper,
> Keeps a-sniffin' for his supper—
> That—old—bear.

Beanie stopped singing. Instead of cheering him up the song had made him hungrier.

He forced himself to start climbing. "This time I'll do it," he said. "I'll do it, I'll do it, I'll *do* it."

He scrabbled and he scratched and he snaked himself up and up and up—clawing with his fingers, scraping with his knees, digging in with his toes.

Now he had fought his way up much higher than before. But

all for nothing, it seemed. He began to slip and slide and slither back again.

His right hand shot up. He grabbed the root of a tree—a root hanging down like a rope. He pulled himself up till his left hand got hold of another root.

Then *tug* and *hoist* and *haul,* he heaved himself into a black-berry bush above the rocks.

Briers were pricking him. He didn't care. He hardly felt them. He just lay panting and resting, glad he had done it, *done* it.

Pretty soon he got up. Going home would be easy, now. He followed gentle slopes and took a long roundabout way downward.

After a while he was under the rocks at the place where his puppy had vanished into the woods.

He hunted here and he hunted there. He hunted all around. "Here puppy," he kept calling. "Here pup, here pup, here pup!"

But he couldn't find his puppy. No. He couldn't.

At last he gave up. He made a new start—toward home. His throat felt tight. His feet felt heavy. Tears in his eyes kept making the woods a green blur.

Long early-morning shadows had turned into fat noonday shadows by the time Beanie saw the Tatum cabin sitting snug and weathered gray in its clearing.

All of a sudden the air was full of noise. Tatum dogs, Sour Bone and Nip and Whizz, were barking and running toward Beanie.

Tatums came hurrying from the cabin—father and mother and Buck and Serena and Irby and Annie Mae.

Barbie and Pinky Nose, the cats, didn't come running, though. They couldn't. They were busy. They were very busy sleeping.

Cookie, the fat cat, did start to come. But she just took three steps and sat down.

The Tatums and the Tatum dogs gave Beanie a wonderful welcome. And Annie Mae kept telling him he had got home in time for his birthday dinner and his great big choc'laty birthday cake.

Beanie didn't say much till his mother's arms were around him. And then he burst right out: "Oh, Ma, I tore my shirt and I tore my overalls and I lost my gun and I lost my cap and I lost my candy and *I lost my puppy.*"

His mother said gently, "Beanie, you haven't lost your puppy. He came home all by himself. He was plumb tuckered out and he's sound asleep, round by the back steps."

"Yip, yip, yip, yip, yip!" came a lot of excited yippings.

"Well!" said Beanie's mother. "Look behind you."

Beanie turned and looked. And there was Tough Enough, himself, running toward him just as fast as he could make his short legs go.

Beanie picked him up and held him close. The puppy licked every bit of Beanie he could reach.

Early that afternoon, Beanie and Tough Enough were on their way to the woodpile. They were full of birthday dinner and choc'laty birthday cake. Tightly and wonderfully full.

Beanie was singing gaily:

Old man he eats the bear,
He eats him smack, smack, smack.
He eats him chomp, chomp, chomp.
He eats him cronch, cronch, cronch.
Old man he eats the bear,
But he's got to shoot him first.
He's a-huntin' for his supper,
Keeps a-huntin' for his supper—
That—old—man.

Beanie picked up some stovewood sticks—all the sticks he could carry. He began to tote them toward the cabin. He was smiling.

He looked back at Tough Enough. The puppy had a twig in his mouth. His proud head was holding it high.

He dropped it close to Beanie's feet, then he lay down on his back. His eyes were dancing. He put up his paws and he put up his stomach and he wiggled them at Beanie.